Not
Opposites

Not better. Not worse. Just different.

Written by **Linda Ragsdale**

Illustrated by **Imodraj**

Always remember to show love, choose peace, and see the beauty in the world around you.

Designed by Flowerpot Press
in Franklin, TN.
www.FlowerpotPress.com
Designer: Stephanie Meyers
Editor: Ashley Rideout
DJS-0909-0147
ISBN: 978-1-4867-0870-3
Made in China/Fabriqué en Chine

There is nothing a Peace Dragon likes better than teaching and learning about peace.

Sometimes differences are not better or worse, or opposites; they're just different. We learn how they can work together for the same goal in the pages of this book.

So come on inside...it's peaceful in here.

Wings.

Arms.

Not better.
Not worse.
Not opposites.
Just different.

Webbed feet.

Wiggly toes.

Not better.
Not worse.
Not opposites.
Just different.

Beak.

Mouth.

Not better.
Not worse.
Not opposites.
Just different.

FRIENDS.

Nose.

Snout.

Hair.

Fur.

Hands.

Paws.

Him.

Different parts for different purposes.
Not better.
Not worse.

Not opposites.
Just different.

Strong.

Tall.

Better for some.
Not better for all.
Just different.

Different is you.
Different is me.
Together, differences work.

Together, but different.
Just right.

Hi! I'm Pax. I'm a Peace Dragon.

My very favorite thing in the entire world is to fly around the world and encourage people to be peacemakers, like in these books. Did you know that everyone can be a peacemaker? If you choose to see, speak, and act through a kind heart and calm thoughts, YOU are a peacemaker! Once you practice, it's easy—and pretty fun, too!

We all have times where we need help choosing peace, such as learning to work with people who are different than we are, or dealing with unkind words that come our way. By reading and thinking about ways to choose kindness or peace before a challenge comes our way, it helps us be prepared to choose peace.

By practicing awesome peaceful solutions, we become examples of love, while building a foundation of peacemaking that will last a lifetime.

Pax

HOW TO ENJOY THIS BOOK:

Everyone has something unique and special they can use to help others. We can use our differences every day to work together and solve problems.

In this story, what did the giraffe have that helped solve a problem? What about the elephant? Flip back through the pictures and notice the ways friends used their differences to help others.

Activity time:

Take a look around you. Each person you see has special talents and interests they can use to help others. Maybe one friend loves to run. Maybe one friend can speak another language. Maybe one friend always has a kind word to share. Take a minute and talk about strengths you notice in those around you.

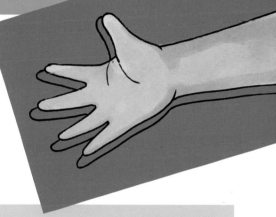

Pass out a piece of paper and marker to each person. Have (or help) children trace and cut out their hands, and write their name on each one. Encourage everyone to walk around the room, and write one thing on each person's hands that they see as unique and special about that person that they could use to help others.

Taking it further:
Make a chain of all of the handprints, by punching two holes in each and stringing them on a piece of yarn. Hang the chain on the wall where everyone can see it, and talk about how when we share our differences and strengths with each other, each of those strengths working together grows into a chain of wonderful things!

Learning through play:

Make a set of animal cards, each with a picture of one of your favorite animals and one of their unique traits. For example, you could draw a picture of a penguin and write, "Can slide on their bellies," or for a bat, "uses sound waves to see in the dark."

After you've made your cards, mix up the deck. Pull out three cards, and make up a story about how those three animals might work together to solve a problem. Maybe they need to cross a river—or even bake a cake! Be as silly as you like!

Taking it further:
What if you made a deck of cards for your family members or your friends? What would you put on your card? How could you all work together?

HOW TO MAKE A PEACE DRAGON:

Using a washable stamp inkpad, use your fingers to make the letter T. Start with a horizontal thumbprint for the dragonhead. To make the body, use your index finger and center and stamp under the thumbprint. To make your dragon fly, stamp the body angled to the side of the head. Add the details to make each dragon unique. Once they're complete, tell a story about your dragon.

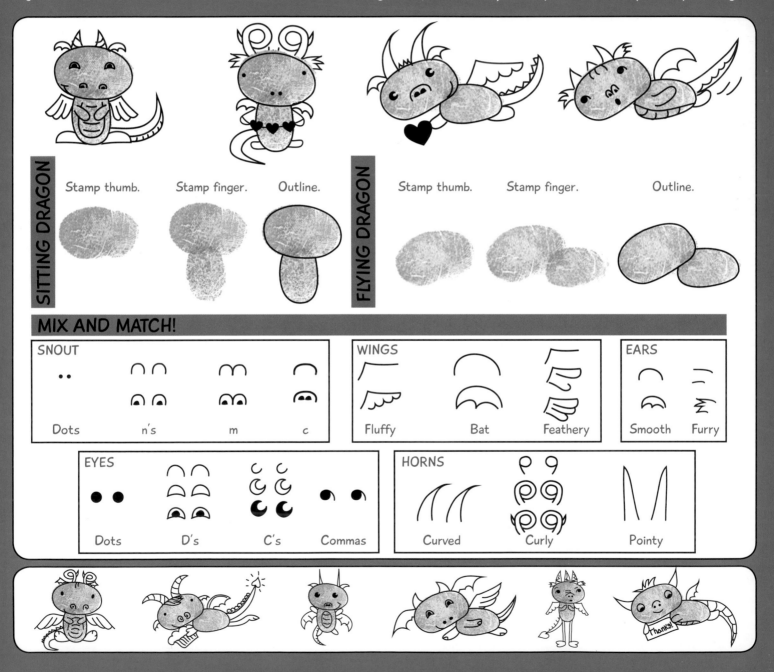

SITTING DRAGON

Stamp thumb.　　Stamp finger.　　Outline.

FLYING DRAGON

Stamp thumb.　　Stamp finger.　　Outline.

MIX AND MATCH!

SNOUT

Dots　　　n's　　　m　　　c

WINGS

Fluffy　　Bat　　Feathery

EARS

Smooth　　Furry

EYES

Dots　　D's　　C's　　Commas

HORNS

Curved　　Curly　　Pointy